D1287656

GRANDMA REMEMBERS

GRANDMA REMEMBERS

story and pictures by Ben Shecter

HARPER & ROW, PUBLISHERS

Grandma Remembers
Copyright © 1989 by Ben Shecter

Library of Congress Cataloging-in-Publication Data
Shecter, Ben.
   Grandma remembers.

  "A Charlotte Zolotow book."
  Summary: A boy and his grandmother take a final tour
of the house she is leaving and relive memories of the
wonderful times experienced there.
  [1. Grandmothers—Fiction]   I. Title.
PZ7.S5382Gr 1989   [E]   88-31986
ISBN 0-06-025617-6
ISBN 0-06-025618-4 (lib. bdg.)

Printed in the U.S.A. All rights reserved.
Typography by Carol Barr
1 2 3 4 5 6 7 8 9 10
First Edition

For Mother

Grandma and I went to say good-bye to the house

where she and Grandpa had lived so long.

"It looks so empty," I said.

"Not empty," she said.

"It's full of memories that we'll always have."

She took my hand in hers,

and we walked from room to room.

In the kitchen she said, "I can still smell the spices.

I remember the rainy days,

the soups simmering, the stews steaming.

The big wooden bowl and the spoon you liked to lick.

The birthday cakes for Grandpa."

"Your stove was always warm," I said.

For I remembered it all, too.

We went through the swinging door to the dining room.

"I remember Thanksgivings," she said.

"You playing with the drumsticks,

and the lace tablecloth we had.

You liked the goblets filled with apple cider."

"I loved the tinkling sound they made

when we toasted each other," I said.

In the parlor Grandma looked out the window.

"Your grandpa and I planted that tree before you were born.

Every Christmas we trimmed it with little lights

and the silver ornaments he made."

"I remember when Grandpa held me on his shoulders

and let me put the star on top," I said.

Grandma smiled.

On the porch Grandma said,

"I remember the spring sounds coming in the open windows,

the birds singing and nesting in the birdhouse that your

father built when he was a boy."

I looked at the birdhouse in the garden.

"It looks new," I said.

"Your grandpa painted it last year," Grandma said,

"but it's the one that your father built."

We walked along the cobblestone path.

The peonies were almost open.

"Look at the delphiniums," said Grandma.

A bushy ground squirrel ran by.

"That's Delbert," she said.

But the squirrel only twitched its tail and scampered off.

Grandma and I went back inside.

We went up the stairs

where the tall clock had been on the landing.

I remembered its slow chimes.

"*Bong, bong, bong,*" I sang.

Grandma laughed.

Upstairs, in the room that had been my father's,

she showed me the secret hiding place he had

when he was little.

I have one too, but I didn't tell her so.

We went into the room that had been Grandpa's and hers.

She told me about the wind in the attic

and the noises they heard at night,

about the curtains making moving shadows on the walls.

"Sometimes I was frightened," she said,

"but Grandpa would say, 'Don't worry. I'm here.'"

Downstairs Grandma took a key out of her pocket.

She locked the front door.

"Now!" she said quietly.

"What?" I asked.

"Off to a new home," she said,

"to see and do and hear new things."

"And if there are noises,"

I said,

"don't worry, Grandma,

I'll be there!"